My First Adventures

W9-DFP-295

MY FIRST TRIP TO THE
DENTIST

By Katie Kawa

Gareth Stevens
Publishing

Please visit our website, www.garethstevens.com. For a free color catalog of all our high-quality books, call toll free 1-800-542-2595 or fax 1-877-542-2596.

Library of Congress Cataloging-in-Publication Data

Kawa, Katie.
My first trip to the dentist / Katie Kawa.
    p. cm. — (My first adventures)
Includes index.
ISBN 978-1-4339-6243-1 (pbk.)
ISBN 978-1-4339-6244-8 (6-pack)
ISBN 978-1-4339-6241-7 (library binding)
1. Dentistry—Juvenile literature. 2. Children—Preparation for dental care—Juvenile literature. I. Title.
RK63.K39 2012
617—dc23

2011016967

First Edition

Published in 2012 by
Gareth Stevens Publishing
111 East 14th Street, Suite 349
New York, NY 10003

Copyright © 2012 Gareth Stevens Publishing

Editor: Katie Kawa
Designer: Haley W. Harasymiw

All illustrations by Planman Technologies

Printed in the United States of America

CPSIA compliance information: Batch #CW12GS: For further information contact Gareth Stevens, New York, New York at 1-800-542-2595.

Contents

Today I am going
to the dentist.

5

The dentist keeps
my teeth healthy.

A man helps my dentist.
He cleans my teeth.

He brushes them.

He takes a picture
of my teeth.
This is called an X-ray.

13

Then I see the dentist.
She looks at my teeth.

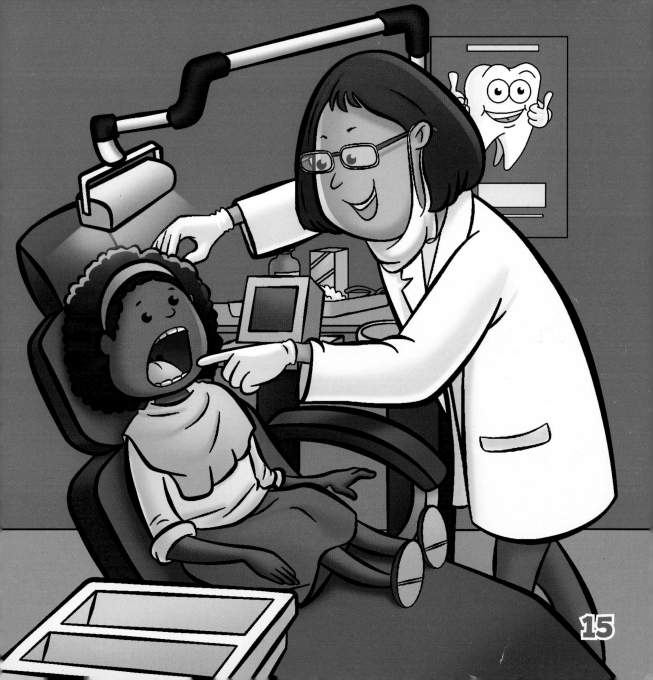

She counts them too.

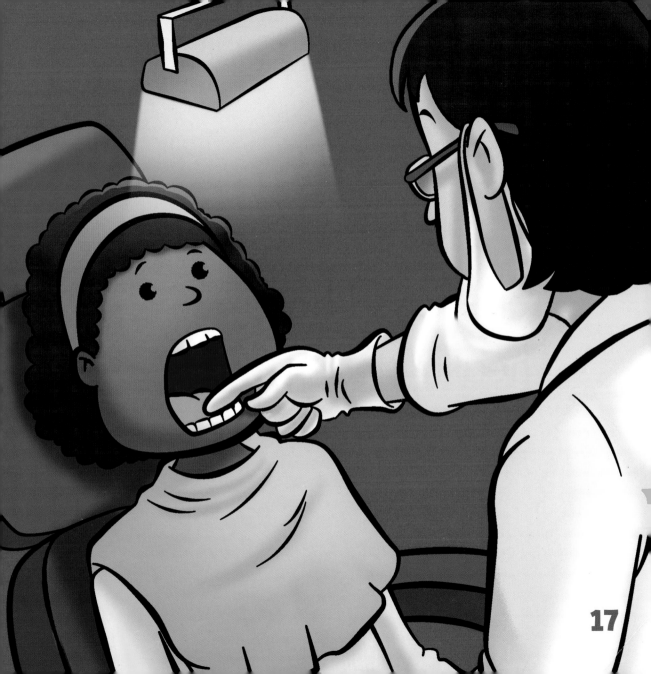

She says I have healthy teeth.

She gives me a sticker!

I love my clean teeth!

Words to Know

sticker

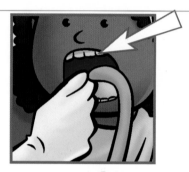

teeth

Index

24